*THE MYSTERY OF THE
DISAPPEARING TAXI*

"Come on, Arabel," said Mr Jones, "I'm
going down to the car-park to look out for
that tea-leaf who's been half-inching my
taxi."

The mystery had begun when Arabel's
dad's taxi started to use more fuel than ever
before. Then when someone reported
seeing it on the Marsh at five in the
morning, Mr Jones and Arabel decide to
keep watch to discover the identity of the
thief – with Mortimer's help, of course.

But one thing leads to another, and soon
Naughty Madge Owens, the Hatmen and
little Mr Beeline from the public library are
all caught up in a crazy adventure.

Joan Aiken
THE MYSTERY OF MR JONES'S DISAPPEARING TAXI

As told in Jackanory

illustrated by Quentin Blake

BBC/KNIGHT BOOKS

Copyright © Joan Aiken Enterprises Ltd 1982
Illustrations © Quentin Blake 1982

First published 1982 by the British Broadcasting
Corporation/Knight Books

British Library C.I.P.

Aiken, Joan
    The mystery of Mr. Jones's disappearing
    taxi.—(Knight books)
    I. Title
    823'.914[J]   PZ7

    ISBN 0-340-27533-2
    ISBN 0-563-17882-5 (BBC)

Printed and bound in Great Britain for
The British Broadcasting Corporation,
35 Marylebone High Street, London W1M 4AA
and Hodder and Stoughton Paperbacks, a
division of Hodder and Stoughton Ltd,
Mill Road, Dunton Green, Sevenoaks, Kent
(Editorial Office: 47 Bedford Square, London,
WC1B 3DP) by Richard Clay (The Chaucer Press) Ltd, Bungay,
Suffolk. Photoset by Rowland Phototypesetting Ltd,
Bury St Edmunds, Suffolk.

1

Things were a bit gloomy in the Jones
household. Firstly, between Guy Fawkes'
day and Christmas there had been only two
days when it hadn't rained. This made
everybody bad-tempered.

Arabel Jones couldn't practise on her new
skateboard.

Mortimer the raven couldn't chase the
next-door cat.

Mrs Jones couldn't stroll about the
shopping precinct with her sister Brenda.

Mr Jones was the only person who didn't
mind the wet weather: people ride in taxis
much more when it is wet, and as he was a
taxi-driver the rain brought him plenty of
customers. But he had a grievance of his
own: the gas men were digging a trench all
the way along Rainwater Crescent, where
the Joneses lived (and being very slow about

it, because their trench kept filling up with rain and having to be pumped out). All the time they were digging the trench, which seemed to have gone on for weeks and weeks, Mr Jones had not been able to park his taxi outside his own front door, but had, instead, to leave it in the car-park at the end of the street. And the result of leaving it in the car-park had been very strange.

"Blest if I know why it is," grumbled Mr Jones one morning at breakfast, "but the old bus seems to use a deal more fuel than she done 'afore."

"Oh, dear, Ben, perhaps you need a new taxi," said Mrs Jones, putting on her coat to go and be a temporary receptionist at a hairdressers' salon for two hours.

"Rubbish, Martha, I've only had this cab five year!" said Mr Jones. "A good taxi can last twenty year, properly looked after, that is."

"P'raps it doesn't *like* being left in the car-park," suggested Arabel.

Just then Chris Cross came to take Arabel to the public library. Arabel had lately become very fond of reading, and as Chris spent a lot of time at the library, because he was working for his college entrance, he had agreed to take Arabel along whenever he went. This suited Mrs Jones, as when Arabel was at the library she could do part-time work for an agency that supplied offices with temporary help. The only problem about this arrangement was Mortimer, Arabel's raven. Mrs Jones flatly refused to leave him alone in the house when she went out, because of the unheard-of damage he was likely to cause if not kept under observation. Mortimer was very fond of eating wire, and had once wrecked the electrical system by chewing up every inch of the wire in the house when Mrs Jones ran out to the shops for five minutes for a cauliflower, taking Arabel with her; while another time he got stuck inside the spin-dryer, causing it to hop all over the floor, overturn the kitchen table, and turn twenty pots of marmalade that Mrs Jones had just made into a shambles of broken glass and squish. Consequently Mrs Jones insisted that Mortimer must accompany Chris and Arabel on their visits to the library. Arabel was always happy to have Mortimer with her, but Miss Acaster the head librarian gave a shudder whenever she saw Mortimer come through the entrance.

"Ready, Arabel?" said Chris Cross. "Got the books you're taking back? You don't need your raincoat today, the forecast said 'Fine and Dry'. Just fancy!"

"Then I'll take my skateboard," said Arabel. She picked it up, as well as *Splendours of the Heavens*, *Freud Explained to the Children*, and *The Bad Child's Book of Beasts*.

"Mind – you're not to go in the road with that skateboard, Arabel dearie," said Mrs Jones.

"No. I'll go under Rumbury Tower Heights," said Arabel.

"And mind you're home sharp at one," said Mrs Jones.

"Yes, Ma," said Arabel, putting on her duffel-coat, which was convenient for Mortimer because he could sit in the hood; and did.

"Mr Jones," said Chris, "isn't the registration of your taxi JON 333 N?"

"Yes, it is," said Mr Jones. "Why?"

"Were you driving about at five this morning?"

"No I most certainly was *not*," said Mr Jones. "Up before seven, dead before eleven. Why?"

"Well, I was up at five because I'm doing temporary post work," said Chris, "and I saw your taxi being driven across Rumbury Marsh."

"You did *what*?" said Mr Jones, his eyes popping.

"Saw your taxi! I ought to know it anyway," said Chris, "I've cleaned it often enough. I recognised the dent in the bumper, let alone the registration."

"Then some so-and-so's half-inching it at night and using it," said Mr Jones, "and *that's* why it's been so heavy on the gas lately! Just wait till I get my hands on the perisher! I'll make him sorry he ever learned to drive! I'll lay for him at the car-park this very night."

"I'll come too," said Chris, "with my motorbike. Then we can follow him and see where he goes."

"Oh yes! I'll come too!" cried Arabel. "And we could put Mortimer inside the taxi – hidden in the glove pouch – then he could pop out presently and give the thief a fright. He'd like that, wouldn't you, Mortimer?"

"KAAARK!" said Mortimer, his eyes shining.

"Well, we'll see, we'll see, we'll see about that," said Mr Jones, not quite certain as to that part of the plan.

Mrs Jones had gone out by this time, or she would undoubtedly have disapproved, very strongly indeed.

Arabel and Chris went off to the library with Mortimer sitting in the hood of Arabel's duffel-coat.

Rumbury Public Library was a handsome new building, built on the edge of Rumbury Marshes and the long road that was called Rumbury Waste. The library was round, like a gasometer, but had many more windows, and there were all sorts of modern gadgets inside. For instance there was a copier. You put 5p in a slot, and then it would copy any letter or picture that you laid under a rubber flap on top. Mortimer used to try to get a copy of himself (whenever Arabel had 5p to spare) – but he could never lie flat enough under the flap to make the copier work properly. Still he loved the bright light and the humming noise it made, and he used to annoy people a good deal, when they were trying to make copies of things, by suddenly rushing up from behind them and diving headfirst under the flap just as the light was shining. Then there was a huge electric index of all the books in the library: you pressed a knob and the names of the books came up on a screen, and you turned another knob which made all the titles roll upwards, right through the

alphabet. Mortimer loved turning the
second knob very fast, and whizzing the
books through from *Aardvarks at Home* to
Zebra-Training for Beginners. But Miss Acaster
was not at all keen on Mortimer doing this.

The various other people who used the
library were never very pleased, either, when
they saw Mortimer come in. His visits nearly
always seemed to end in some kind of
disturbance; he liked to climb on the trolley
where the returned books were stacked, and
shove it along with his wings at a fearful
speed; or he flew up to the gallery where the
reference books were kept, and dropped
dictionaries over the rail on to people's
heads; or he just climbed around from one

shelf to another, muttering loudly to himself, and sometimes shouting, "Nevermore!" in a very loud and distracting way.

Mortimer was not a restful bird.

There was one little man, however, who was always delighted to see Arabel and Mortimer come into the library; his name was Mr Beeline. We shall return to him later.

On this particular morning Miss Acaster walked over to Arabel very fast, as soon as she came in. "We are always happy to see *you*, my dear," Miss Acaster said firmly, "but your bird must stay outside."

"Oh, but please, he *always* comes in," said Arabel. "I don't think he'd be happy if he was left outside! And when he's unhappy he gets cross, and when he's cross he does things that are inconvenient."

"He is *just* as inconvenient *inside*," said Miss Acaster. "I'm afraid he must stay out. A new regulation has been passed by the library committee, and it is to be strictly enforced."

She pointed to a card that said:

NO RAVENS IN THE LIBRARY.
BY ORDER.

"Oh dear," said Arabel. "Well, in that case, Mortimer, I'm afraid you'll have to

stay out on the terrace. I'll be as quick as I can."

Strangely enough, Mortimer did not seem too upset at being made to wait outside. He sat on the open stone terrace and looked across Rumbury Marshes at a huge high-rise building that had been put up there a couple of years before. It was called Rumbury Tower Heights. Mortimer seemed very interested in it.

When Arabel had chosen her books – *Mathematics for Moppets*, *Advanced Skateboarding*, and *Flower-Fairies of the Autumn*, she came to the counter to have them stamped.

She heard two of the librarians talking together.

"It wouldn't surprise *me* if it was that raven that was responsible for all the books that have been stolen from the library in the last six months," said Mr Trigg, the under-librarian. "Over a thousand books! It's scandalous!"

Arabel was indignant. "Mortimer has never stolen a single book!" she said. "He does like to *eat* books, I know, but I don't let him. He has never eaten a single library book."

"Well I'm glad to hear it," said Mr Trigg, but he did not sound as if he believed Arabel.

"I'll be outside," Arabel whispered to Chris, who was reading at a table. He nodded and she went out. On the terrace, Mortimer was still gazing at Rumbury Tower Heights.

"Shall we go over there and skate, Mortimer?" said Arabel.

There was a bit of grassy, weedy waste ground between the library and the tower building. It was always damp, because it was really Rumbury Marsh. Nobody wanted to build anything on it, because it flooded every winter, sooner or later – and sometimes in the summer too.

Arabel walked over the soggy grass (luckily she was wearing gumboots) to the tower building. It was twenty stories high, and stood on twelve legs. Underneath, in among the legs, was a wide stretch of concrete pavement, just right for skateboards. In the middle of the pavement was a fountain. This was like a stone tank, about the length of two buses standing end to end. All along inside the tank, jets of water shot up. They were quite high – in fact they shot as high as the ceiling, which was the underside of the tower block. Arabel was very fond of the fountain. She stood looking at it for a long time. So did Mortimer. First one jet would slowly let itself down until it was almost gone. Then it would shoot up again, higher and higher, till it hit the ceiling. Then the next one would do the same thing.

"Wouldn't it be lovely to sit on one of those jets, Mortimer," Arabel said, as she always did.

"Kaaaark," said Mortimer, as he always did.

Then Arabel carefully put down the plastic bag containing her library books. She put her skateboard on the ground, got on to it, pushed herself off with one foot, and went gliding away. She wove a complicated course in between the twelve thick pillars that held the tower block above her, winding in and out, going round and round the fountain. Mortimer rode happily in the hood of her duffel-coat, singing a one-word, one-note song to himself, over and over. It went: "Nevermore. Nevermore. Never, never, never, never, never, nevermore."

They were the only people there.

Nobody lived in Rumbury Tower Heights, or worked there. A firm had built the block three years before, and advertised it for office and business premises, but they had asked such enormous rents that no one wanted to use the building and it stood empty.

Six months ago there had been an indignant headline in the *Rumbury Gazette*: RUMBURY TOWER STILL STANDS EMPTY. WHY DOES NOT THE COUNCIL STEP IN?

Actually the ones who had stepped in were a colony of bats, who had discovered it and nested there; they liked it because most of the windows were shuttered, which made a comfortable darkness for them. Professor

Pook, a very learned natural historian, had been to look at the bats, and got very excited about them because they were a rare and large species, not usually found in England. He had the whole building declared a Bat Sanctuary. Now nobody was supposed to go into it at all, for fear of disturbing the bats, except a building inspector, who looked in once a month to make sure the place was safe and not likely to fall down. And *he* stayed no longer than he absolutely had to.

"Proper spooky it is, I'm glad to get out of there, I can tell you," he said. "Fustly there's no power, no lights, no heat, no lift, you has to walk up all them stairs and it's as cold and dark as the inside of a deep-freeze. And, second, there's all them blinkin' bats hanging upside down looking right nasty – some of them have got a wing-spread of over five foot, I give you my word."

Indeed Professor Pook said this was quite possible, as they were Kalong bats from the East Indies; no doubt they had arrived in Rumbury Dock on some fruit boat.

Mortimer loved scooting around in Arabel's hood underneath the tower block, as he had very sharp ears, and he could hear the bats squeaking and snoring up above. He often planned to visit the bats; but he had not yet found out how to get into Rumbury Tower Heights. He was still thinking about this project.

Other people were also interested in visiting Rumbury Tower Heights.

"There comes Chris," Arabel said presently. "Time to go home, Mortimer."

"Kaaark," said Mortimer, staring thoughtfully up at the top of the fountain jets, where they hit the roof.

He was very silent all the way home in Arabel's hood.

2

That evening, when Mr Jones came in, he said, "I've decided to do what young Chris said."

"What's that, Ben?" Mrs Jones asked. However, just at that moment, the part-time job agency phoned to ask if Mrs Jones could go round to the offices of Rumbury Pirate Radio for a couple of hours, as their receptionist had gone home with a nosebleed.

Mrs Jones put on her coat and went off, reminding Arabel and her father that Arabel's bedtime was eight-thirty sharp.

Mr Jones glanced out of the window. It was as dark outside as the inside of a gumboot, but it was not raining, nor particularly cold; he said, "Come on, Arabel; I'm going down to the car-park to look out for that tea-leaf who's been half-inching my taxi."

"Oh yes!" said Arabel with enthusiasm, and she ran to put on her duffel-coat again, and tucked Mortimer into the hood. They stopped at the Cross house (which was next door) and invited Chris to come along too, which he did, scooting on his motorbike beside them.

When they got to the car-park they could see that Mr Jones's taxi was in its usual spot, right at this end, near the turnstile, which was left open at night.

"So the thief hasn't been yet," said Chris.

"Do let's put Mortimer inside," said Arabel. "Then he can give the thief a terrible fright, can't you, Mortimer."

"Kaark," said Mortimer.

"But," objected Mr Jones, "suppose he gives him such a fright that the guy runs my taxi into a lamp-post and dents it?"

However in the end Mr Jones was persuaded to allow Mortimer to get into the taxi and hide in the glove-pouch; firstly because he said, "That bird might as well make himself useful somehow; dear knows he eats enough"; and secondly because after they had waited half an hour or so, hiding behind the hedge, Mortimer began to be a bit of a nuisance, grumbling and shouting

"Nevermore", and Mr Jones was afraid he might give away the ambush. So Mortimer was put into the glove pocket and told to keep quiet.

Inside the glove pocket, Mortimer promptly fell asleep.

The watchers did not have long to wait (luckily, for the clock on Rumbury Town Hall was visible from where they were hiding and Arabel could see that it said 8.45). A small dark figure slipped along between the lines of cars, unlocked the door of Mr Jones's taxi ("Cor!" whispered Mr Jones, "the son-of-a-gun must have had a duplicate key made!"), started up the motor, and drove away rapidly, along Canal Road.

Immediately, Chris Cross threw a leg over his motorbike; Mr Jones, holding Arabel, got on the pillion behind him; and Chris started up his engine. None too soon; for the taxi-lights were almost out of sight.

Chris was after it in a flash; and Mr Jones had plenty of time to regret his decision to allow Arabel to come with them. "Martha will never forgive me for this," he groaned to himself, as the motorbike wound swiftly in and out of traffic, shot over zebra crossings and traffic lights, needled its way through

tiny gaps, whizzed across roundabouts, zipped between level-crossing gates, and bounded over bridges. The thief seemed to be joyriding all over Rumbury Town.

Arabel was having the time of her life. "I'm sorry Mortimer's missing this," she thought. "It's even better than skateboarding. When I'm bigger, I'll get a motorbike just like Chris's."

"Have we lost the perisher?" yelled Mr Jones to Chris.

"I think he went this way," Chris yelled back over his shoulder.

He was now going in the direction of Rumbury Public Library. However when they reached it, there was no taxi to be seen.

"Hey, what's that, then?" said Chris.

There was a light crossing the marsh. Chris accelerated, and zipped along the side of Rumbury Waste. Then he turned left.

"*Is* that him, ahead?"

"Yeah, yeah," said Chris. "I think so."

"Is he driving natural, like?" said Mr Jones, who couldn't see much, because Chris's crash helmet was in the way.

"Seems to be," said Chris.

"Mortimer can't have let out his squawk yet," said Mr Jones.

"Maybe he's biding his time," said Chris.

Some traffic lights ahead of them turned red; they had to wait. "Funny thing," said Chris, peering ahead. "Taxi seems to have stopped under the big tower – Rumbury Heights. What's he want to go there for?"

By the time Chris had come to a halt under the tower, where Arabel had been skating earlier in the day, the taxi was parked quietly beside the fountain. But there was nobody inside it. No thief – and no Mortimer either. The glove pouch was empty.

"Oh my goodness," Arabel said anxiously. "What can have happened to Mortimer?"

They all hunted about, among the pillars and behind the fountain. Nobody was there.

Arabel came back to the fountain and studied it thoughtfully. It was still fountaining, because it ran on solar heat, charging up enough energy in the daytime to keep it going all night. The jets of water looked very handsome, dyed bright yellow by the rays from the street lights along Rumbury Waste.

Mr Jones and Chris were planning to lurk by the taxi until the thief reappeared. "Then we can catch him red-handed," said Mr Jones. "But I suppose he may be a long time, if you saw him driving home at five in the morning," he added doubtfully, looking at Chris. "Arabel, dearie, maybe you'd better get into the cab. Then you can have a nap, see, and keep warm – and you'll be out o' the way, if there's any ruckus."

But there was no answer from Arabel, and, looking round, Mr Jones saw with alarm that she, too, had disappeared.

Meanwhile Mrs Jones, round at the offices of Rumbury Pirate Radio, was having an interesting time. Rumbury Pirate Radio was run from a barge which was moored in the middle of Rumbury Canal, just where it ran into the River Thames; you reached the barge by going across a gangway, which made Mrs Jones rather nervous. However, once inside, it seemed much like any other office; Mrs Jones sat at a pink desk with a bunch of gladiolus on it and a sign that said *Inquiries*. Her job was to answer the phone, and direct visitors where they should go. The agency had told Mrs Jones that she was lucky to get this job, as she might see all kinds of celebrities, such as The Rocking Horses, or Foul Fred Fink, or Tuppenny Rice, or the Sewer Rats. But, as Mrs Jones wasn't interested in pop music and knew nothing whatever about rock or punk, she might not have recognised Foul Fred Fink even if she had seen him.

In fact there were not many celebrities tonight. It was rather quiet. Mrs Jones got a

whole sleeve of a cardigan knitted for
Arabel. Then the phone rang, and Mrs
Jones, picking up the receiver, said:
"Rumbury Pirate Radio, can I help you?"

A low thick fierce voice hissed in her ear.
It said: "Listen! We are the Hatmen! We
have got Naughty Madge Owens, who is
being kept in a secret hideaway where no
one will ever think of searching. If a ransom
of eight million pounds is not paid by next
Thursday January the tenth, she will be
weighted with twelve volumes of the *Complete
Oxford Dictionary* and dropped into the
Rumbury Canal."

"*What!*" shrieked Mrs Jones.

"Eight million pounds for the return of Naughty Madge Owens! The money must be put into plastic garbage bags and left in the builders' rubbish skip that is standing outside the deserted asbestos factory near Rumbury Dock. Is that clear?"

"No!" gasped Mrs Jones. But the caller had rung off.

Mrs Jones immediately went into hysterics. She laughed, she cried, she wailed, she gurgled, she hiccuped, she screamed, she gibbered.

Quite soon, people began to come out of their offices, and ask her what was the matter.

"Oh!" wept Mrs Jones. "They want eight million pounds put in plastic bags and taken to the asbestos factory. But how can we collect even *one* million pounds, let alone eight?"

"But *who* want eight million? And why? And where is the asbestos factory? What is this all about, Mrs Jones?"

"Those fiends have got our raven!"

"For heaven's sake, what fiends?"

"How should *I* know what fiends?" sobbed Mrs Jones, rocking to and fro. "How should I know what horrible criminals have taken it into their wicked heads to go off with him, or why? But they've *got* him, that's for sure. Plain as I'm sitting here the disgusting wretch said, 'We have got Mortimer Jones!' And if they've got Mortimer, they *must* have Arabel too!''

Then she fainted dead away.

All the people at Rumbury Pirate Radio were very concerned for her, and they rushed about, burning feathers under her nose (fortunately there were plenty of these, because of the plentiful seagulls always perching in the rigging and on the aerial and upsetting reception and dropping feathers on the deck); they also undid Mrs Jones's collar and slapped her hands and gave her brandy and sal volatile to drink.

Of course it was pure bad luck for the kidnappers of Naughty Madge Owens that their phone message had been received by Mrs Jones. She was very likely the only person in Rumbury Town (or indeed in London) – not counting Mortimer, that is – who had never heard of the famous pop singer. Naughty Madge Owens had been born plain Margaret in Walton-on-the-Naze and rechristened herself Naughty Madge when she became a singer. She had a huge and devoted fan club, several million strong, who would certainly have been happy to subscribe to the ransom. Eight million pounds would have been nothing to them. But because of Mrs Jones's mistake, the news of Naughty Madge's abduction never got out.

When Mrs Jones had recovered a little, the kind-hearted supervisor drove her home. But a lot of time was wasted because Mrs Jones was gulping and choking so much that the supervisor thought she said she lived in Rayners' Lane, not Rainwater Crescent.

When she finally did get home, Mrs Jones was not surprised to find the house dark and empty. "Very likely the kidnappers have taken Ben, too," she tearfully said. "I'd better phone up my cousin Sam."

"Yes, you do that, dear," the supervisor kindly said. "And I'll stay till he comes."

Actually Mrs Jones's cousin Sam Halliwell was a Detective Sergeant in Rumbury Police, and as soon as she had got him on the phone, Mrs Jones screeched at him: "Sam, Sam, some horrible kidnappers have gone off with our Mortimer, and probably little Arabel and Ben too, leastways nobody's at home, and they are

going to drop Mortimer into Rumbury
Canal weighted down with the Oxford
Dictionary – in fact he's probably lying
there already with his toes turned up, for
we've not got the eight million nor likely to
have it! So, please, Sam, please, please drag
the canal *at once*! Oh I don't know what poor
little Arabel will say, unless she's in the
canal too, she'll just about break her heart."

Now of course Cousin Sam was not at all
likely to have the Rumbury Canal dragged
simply on the say-so of his Cousin Martha,
who had been known to get things wrong
before, but in fact the Rumbury Police had
received a tip-off that a gang called the
Hatmen, who had started operating in the
Rumbury area, might have sunk a
consignment of stolen marshmallows in
the canal, sealed in plastic containers.
Accordingly, Sam said: "Well, Martha, we'll

see what we can do. Where are you now?"

"I'm at home," wept Mrs Jones.

"Well, you better stay right at home in case there's violence."

By now it was well into the middle of the night. Mrs Jones hadn't the heart to go to bed, so she made herself a cup of tea and started knitting the second sleeve of Arabel's cardigan.

And, meanwhile, where *was* Naughty Madge Owens?

She had been snatched by the Hatmen. (The gang were called this because they all wore such extremely large hats that their faces were never seen.) They had recently come to England from the south of France, where they had read about the empty condition of Rumbury Tower Heights, in the overseas edition of the *Daily Mail* (which had not, however, mentioned the bats). The Hatmen had got Naughty Madge imprisoned on the eighth floor of Rumbury Tower Heights, and they felt confident that they were going to make a lot of money from her. And they felt certain that Rumbury Tower Heights was going to make a very useful centre of operations.

3

Meanwhile, what had happened to Arabel?

While Mr Jones and Chris, underneath the tower block, were inspecting the empty taxi for marks of violence, and not finding any, Arabel had noticed a small dark figure softly wheeling a trolley into the dim distance. She quietly followed this figure, and getting closer to him, unobserved, noticed with interest that he was little Mr Beeline from the public library! He was the person who always sat reading at a table in the corner, and had directed some particularly nasty looks at Mortimer; moreover his trolley, the sort they have in supermarkets, was quite full of books. Arabel, very curious, followed Mr Beeline and watched him get inside Rumbury Tower Heights by a very clever way.

There was a fire-escape of openwork iron steps, going zigzag right up the side of the building to the top. But it didn't quite reach the ground, in order to prevent burglars making use of it. The bottom flight of steps was like a ladder on a spring; and as long as somebody was not actually *on* it, weighing it down, it swung up and stuck out sideways, eighteen feet up in the air, out of reach of anybody standing on the ground.

Mr Beeline, however, had an umbrella with a telescopic stalk; he calmly pulled the handle out until it was long enough to reach up to the sideways ladder, and used the crook end to pull the steps down. Then he

took the huge bundle of books from his trolley (they were tied together with a rubber strap) and disappeared up the steps, staggering slightly under the weight of his load. When he went inside, the steps sprang back to their original position.

"Well I never!" thought Arabel. "So *he's* the thief who takes all the books from the library! And he uses Pa's taxi to bring them here! If I can find where he puts the books, I'll tell Miss Acaster, and then she'll be so pleased that perhaps she'll let Mortimer into the library again."

Occupied by this interesting plan, Arabel picked up Mr Beeline's umbrella, which he had left lying by the empty trolley, hooked down the steps in her turn, and followed Mr Beeline. She had a strong suspicion, also, that Mortimer had somehow managed to get into the building, and she hoped that she might come across him.

And what *had* happened to Mortimer?

By the time Mr Beeline had driven away the taxi, Mortimer, curled up in the glove pouch, was fast asleep. He woke up at the library, where Mr Beeline halted to pick up the books he had previously hidden in a concrete litter bin. Mortimer was so interested when a large load of books was put in the back that he wasted no time shouting "Nevermore" to scare the driver, but just quietly ate the first three volumes of Edward Gibbon's *Decline and Fall of the Roman Empire*. These lasted him as far as Rumbury Tower Heights. Mr Beeline never noticed Mortimer and he quietly slipped from the taxi while Mr Beeline was unloading his books, and walked over to the fountain.

For a long time, Mortimer had been wondering if it would be possible to sit on top of one of the fountain jets. The present time seemed a very good opportunity to try. While Mr Beeline was wheeling trolley-loads of books back and forth to the fire-escape, Mortimer clambered up the side of the stone tank which held the fountain, and waited until one of the end jets sank down as low as it would go. Then, as it started to rise again, Mortimer launched himself out with his wings – hop, flap – and landed exactly on top of the jet, which was so powerful that it did indeed begin to carry him up. Higher and higher went Mortimer.

"Kaaark!" he said joyfully. It was exactly like sitting on top of a rapidly growing palm

tree. The fountain was rather cold
underneath him, to be sure, but Mortimer
did not mind that – his feathers were so
thick and waterproof that the drops could
not get through to his skin.

Up and up he went, nearly to the ceiling.
And now, just above him, he could see a
little trap-hole which was a ventilator in the
floor of the bottom storey of Rumbury
Tower Heights. Mortimer grabbed the
grating with his beak and claws, and then he
managed to poke his way through between
the bars.

So, at this time, both Arabel and Mortimer were in Rumbury Tower Heights.

Meanwhile, down below, Mr Jones and Chris were becoming more and more anxious and alarmed, hunting far and wide among the pillars and on the grassy ground beyond, calling and calling: "Arabel! Mortimer! Where the devil are you? Where have you got to?"

"Oh, my goodness," said Mr Jones, worried and guilty. "What Martha will say when she hears about this, I do not know." Actually he did know, quite well. Or at least he had a pretty good idea.

Mr Jones and Chris were so perturbed and distracted, wondering where Arabel and Mortimer had got to, that neither of them noticed three dark figures who arrived quietly and unobtrusively on bicycles, parked their bikes against one of the big pillars, pulled a lot of complicated equipment out of their saddlebags, and then proceeded to disappear *up* the pillar with a good deal of whispering, shushing, and giggling. Nor did Mr Jones and Chris hear the mournful baying of a bloodhound in the distance.

But they did notice a police-car, which drew up beside them presently, flashing its blue beacon-light.

"Good heavens! Ben Jones, whatever are *you* doing out here at this hour of night?" asked the police driver, whose name was Roger Mulvey. He lived in Rainwater Crescent, and his sons Bill and Dave were friends of Chris, and he used to play darts with Mr Jones on Thursday evenings.

"Some slimy so-and-so half-inched my cab and brought it out here," said Mr Jones. "And now I've been and gone and lost Arabel."

"Well, she's not here – anyone can see that," said Roger Mulvey, shining his torch round the huge empty space underneath Rumbury Tower Heights. The moon had risen by now, and it shone clean through from side to side. Nobody was there.

"And *you* can't stay," Roger went on. "My orders are to warn everybody and get them cleared out of this area."

"Why?" said Mr Jones rather grumpily. He did not feel that Roger was being as helpful as a policeman ought to be.

"Why? Because the Detective Branch was dragging Rumbury Canal for some reason, and the silly lubbers went and pulled the plug out of the bottom of the canal, and all the water's run away. Like a bath."

"Run away? Where to?"

"Well, these here Rumbury Marshes are the lowest part of the town, so the water's just naturally bound to turn up here before long. Any minute now there'll be a big flood. In fact – " he pointed – "there it comes *now*, so you better get in your cab and scarper."

"But what about Arabel?" Mr Jones was horrified. "And Mortimer?"

"Well, you can see they aren't here," said Roger, reasonably. "So get a move on!" And he went whizzing off with his blue lights flashing to warn any other people who might be out on Rumbury Marsh in the moonlight.

Now Mr Jones and Chris could see quite a lot of water pouring across the marsh, shining like icing-sugar, so Mr Jones leapt into his taxi and Chris sprang on to his motorbike, and they, too, shot away to the higher land by the public library and the gas works. And in ten minutes Rumbury Tower Heights, standing on its twelve legs, was marooned in the middle of a great swashing inland sea, twenty feet deep, in which a lot of marshmallows were bobbing about.

Mr Jones and Chris, nearly mad with worry, could think of nothing better to do than go back to Number Six Rainwater Crescent, in case by some lucky chance Arabel and Mortimer had managed to get home before them. But of course all they found was Mrs Jones knitting and having hysterics.

"Mortimer and Arabel's been kidnapped by a Dictionary Gang," she wailed at them. "And Cousin Sam's out dragging the canal for them this very minute, so *you'd* better get a boat and start looking too."

Chris and Mr Jones gazed at each other glumly. They could get no more sense out of Mrs Jones (if what she had said so far could be called sense), so her husband put her to bed with a cup of tea and a Dormodol pill.

"My mate Sandy's got a dinghy with an outboard," said Chris thoughtfully. "Maybe Mrs Jones has got a point. We could borrow Sandy's dinghy and go out on the floods in it, for a look-round."

Mr Jones could find no fault with this plan, so they went along to the Smith house, which was also in Rainwater Crescent. Mr Smith was not best pleased at being woken at four in the morning, which it was by now, with a request for his son's dinghy, but when he heard that there was a flood, and that Arabel Jones was missing, he became more helpful.

"Sandy's not here – he's staying the night with a couple of pals of his, Bill and Dave Mulvey – but he'd certainly let you have the boat. It's in the garden – help yourself."

So Chris and Mr Jones put the boat on top of Mr Jones's taxi and drove back from Rainwater Crescent towards Rumbury Waste.

4

Meanwhile, what had happened to
Mortimer?

He had been very interested indeed to find
himself inside Rumbury Tower Heights.
Because no one had ever made use of it, the
building was not furnished at all. There were
hundreds of big empty rooms and long
empty passages. There were two lifts in the
middle, which were not working because
there was no power, and there were
escalators, all the way from the first floor to
the twentieth, which were also stationary,
like ordinary stairs with a smooth handrail
on each side. Mortimer had an enjoyable
time for half an hour or so climbing up some
flights of the escalator and then sliding down
the handrail, shouting "Nevermore!" at the
top of his voice.

Since the building was not furnished, there were no carpets on the floors or curtains over the windows, it was all bare and echoing, it carried sound particularly well, and Mortimer's shouts rang from the first floor to the twentieth, sounding like the Day of Judgment. This soon disturbed the bats, who had taken up residence on the fourth floor. They began to squeak and flap, and to drop off the picture-rails where they were hanging in large black clumps like bunches of grapes, and to fly around the building, going all the way up and down the centre well, where the escalator was, and along the passages.

Mortimer became tremendously excited when the bats came out. They were a great deal bigger than he was, with wide leathery wings, long snouts, tiny eyes, sharp teeth, and big complicated ears. They had a claw on each hand, but were not really fierce; they were rather gentle simple creatures who lived on fruit when they could get it, but as they could not get fruit in Rumbury Tower Heights, had to make do with spiders and earwigs. Mortimer was not in the least afraid of the bats, although there were such a lot of them; he began to chase them about, shouting "Nevermore." He even flew – a thing he was not fond of doing. The poor bats grew very flustered indeed – they had never come across anything like Mortimer – they circled wildly about the building, squeaking and shrilling and flapping their wings with a noise like washing in a high wind.

And this disturbance of the bats had other unexpected results.

The first was that five rather short men in black cloaks and extremely large hats suddenly erupted from a room on the eighth floor and fled in terrible disarray along one of the corridors, shrieking: "Dio mio! Allegro ma non troppo! Cosi fan tutte! Vampires, vampires!" at the tops of their voices.

They passed clean by Arabel, without noticing her, in their terror and confusion; Arabel had been going steadily through the building, floor by floor, looking for Mortimer in the moonlight which came through the Venetian blinds on the windows. There was such a lot of fuss and commotion going on in the building that she felt sure Mortimer must be somewhere not far off.

The Hatmen – for these five men were the fiendish Mediterranean gang who had kidnapped Naughty Madge Owens – went careering down one of the stationary escalators, tripping, stumbling, and falling over one another. Their progress down the escalator was not helped by the fact that piles of books were stacked on every step. At the bottom, on the seventh floor, they were brought to a stop by a massive rampart of books. Filippo Fedora, the leader of the gang, was in front, and hit the pile of books at such speed that the whole enormous heap toppled over on the rest of the gang as they came barrelling down, knocking them all unconscious.

Arabel had not observed this, for she heard a voice crying: "Help! Help!" The voice seemed to be coming from the room

out of which the Hatmen had dashed so
hastily. Arabel went in, to see who was
calling, and there she found Naughty Madge
Owens, tied by her hands and legs to a chair,
and looking very indignant.

A lot of bats were flying around overhead.

"Shall I untie you?" said Arabel.

"Yes, do, for goodness sake!" said
Naughty Madge Owens. She was as skinny
as a broom-handle, with very pale cheeks,
and flashing blue eyes, and extremely white
teeth, and a huge mop of shiny black curls,
like a bolster on her head. She said: "I want
to take off my wig, before the bats nest in it.

And I can't do that with my hands tied."

As soon as Arabel had untied her, Madge lifted off the wig, underneath which she had quite short straight hair, about the same length as a wire-haired terrier. "That's better!" she remarked.

In fact the bats showed no wish to nest in her wig, but, as she said, "You can't be too careful, and that wig cost a fortune."

She put the wig carefully in her enormous handbag.

"Aren't you Naughty Madge Owens?" asked Arabel, who often listened to Rumbury Pirate Radio and watched *Top of the Pops*.

"Yes I am, and I can't *think* why nobody's rescued me before, you'd think *somebody* would have started wondering where I was by now, I was due to sing on Rumbury Radio this evening and dear knows I've enough fans – where are they all?" said Madge Owens, still rather crossly. "Not that I don't mean to say ta ever so to you, ducks, for I certainly do! Let's get out of here while those rotten skunks of Hatmen are out of the way, shall we?"

"We can go down the fire escape," said Arabel, for a door led out to it from the room where Madge Owens had been imprisoned. But when they stepped out on to the fire-escape they were very startled indeed to see that Rumbury Tower Heights was now standing in the middle of a lagoon that shone all misty and silvery in the moonlight.

"Coo!" said Arabel. "It wasn't like that before! I wonder when that happened." And then she said: "Oh dear, I do hope Pa and Chris are all right."

At that moment the attention of Arabel and Madge Owens was attracted by a sound close beside them. What was their surprise and curiosity at seeing three people who were occupied in climbing up the wall of Rumbury Tower Heights. The climbers had pitons, iron pegs which they knocked into the concrete wall and then used to pull themselves up. They all carried large bundles on their backs.

"Hullo, Arabel," said one of them. He proved to be Sandy Smith, from Number Eight, Rainwater Crescent. "What are *you* doing here?" he said.

"What are *you*?" said Arabel.

"Bill and Dave and me are the founder members of the R.C.C., that's the Rumbury Climbers' Club," said Sandy, continuing to climb. "We're going up to the top."

"We'll come and meet you there," said Arabel.

She and Naughty Madge did not use the climbers' pitons to get to the top of the building. They merely walked up the fire-escape. By now the pink light of dawn was beginning to creep into the sky. It was a fine view, over the surging flood, towards the public library and the gasworks, with the Town Hall in the background.

A cool wind was blowing, and Madge put her wig back on, as the bats were all downstairs. "I'd certainly like to know why my fans haven't come to rescue me," she said again.

Of course many of her fans, still asleep in bed, did not even know yet that she was missing, but they soon would when they got up and read the headlines in the *Rumbury Daily News*: POP STAR FAILS TO SHOW FOR RUMBURY RADIO – WHERE IS NAUGHTY MADGE?

Sandy, Dave and Bill had reached the top, pulled a lot of equipment from their packs, and were slotting it together.

"What are those?" asked Arabel.

"Hang gliders," said Sandy. "Bill and

Dave and I are founder members of the
R.H.G.C. – the Rumbury Hang Gliders'
Club. Cor!" he said, gazing at Madge.
"Aren't you Naughty Madge Owens? Come
on, then, Madgie – give us a song!"

"I will," said Madge, "if you'll give us a
lift down in one of those things. Can you take
a passenger?"

The three boys looked at each other.

"Never tried," said Sandy.

"*Might* be OK," said Dave.

"No harm in having a bash," said Bill.
"After all, they can only go *down*, can't
they?"

So they went on fitting their gliders
together, and Madge opened her mouth and
sang at the top of her tremendously powerful
lungs, the song that had first got her to
Number Two in the charts:
"Evil, idle Isidore,
Every day I love him, more and more
He's evil – he's idle
Downright homicidal
He's my guru and my idol
My love for him is tidal
He's the only guy that I adore!
Evil, evil, idle, idle Isidore!
Every day I idolise him, more and more
He's so evil – so idle
That hunting far and wide'll
Never find another guy like Isidore!"

Madge's voice carried like a peal of bells over the floods. Some people rowing around in boats down below looked up, and began shouting. Some people began to gather along the dry land, over Rumbury Waste.

Meanwhile, what was happening downstairs?

Mortimer had become bored by chasing the bats, and was sitting thoughtfully munching up the OWL to POL volume of the encyclopedia, staring at the Hatmen, who were still lying unconscious among piles of books.

Mortimer was beginning to pine for Arabel, which he did whenever they had been apart for more than a couple of hours.

Suddenly he heard the sound of feet coming up the stairs – one pair of human feet, and the pit-pat of four dog's paws.

Into sight up the stationary escalator came the tall, commanding figure of Miss Acaster the head librarian. She was being pulled along by a large bloodhound on a lead. The bloodhound was woofling with great excitement and interest, and it made a beeline for the feet of Mr Beeline, which were sticking out from under a pile of foreign dictionaries. They had fallen on him when the Hatmen hurtled down in their mad descent.

Miss Acaster was surprised at the sight of Mortimer, and even more so when she noticed all the unconscious Hatmen. But she nodded grimly when the bloodhound dug out Mr Beeline from his pile of books.

"Caught red-handed, selling his loot to a gang of receivers," she remarked. She had been suspicious of Mr Beeline for some weeks, having noticed that he always seemed fatter when he left the library than when he entered it.

She had borrowed Rollo, the bloodhound, from her brother, who bred bloodhounds, and used him to track down Mr Beeline, arriving at Rumbury Tower Heights just five minutes before the flood. Rollo could not possibly have managed the fire-escape, but fortunately Miss Acaster's brother was also the architect who built Rumbury Tower Heights, and he had told her about a concealed door in one of the legs that supported the building, and had given her a key. The door opened on to a spiral stair, leading up inside the leg. In fact the Hatmen had got in that way too, and had left the door open, which was lucky for Miss

Acaster; she and Rollo just got in before the flood. But it had taken them a long time to toil up the spiral stair.

Now Miss Acaster went round in a businesslike way, checking the piles of books, which were all from Rumbury Library. Then she stapled all the Hatmen to the floor, by the wide brims of their hats. (She had brought a staple-gun with her, in case Mr Beeline turned violent). While she was doing this, Mr Beeline began to come to, and peered feebly out from under the dictionaries. He saw Mortimer sitting on the stair-rail, and said venomously: "There! Didn't I say that it was that raven that was stealing the library books?"

"Rubbish, Mr Beeline," replied Miss Acaster. "You should not try to pin the blame on an innocent bird. I have been following you on my bicycle. Furthermore I saw you tuck *Mrs Beeton's Household Management* into the waistband of your trousers before you left the library." She tapped the waistband, which gave out a sound like a brick wall. *Mrs Beeton's Household Management* was still inside. Despite Mr Beeline's protests, Miss Acaster stapled him to the floor by his trousers and sleeves, alongside the rest of the criminals.

"But I don't know anything about *them*," he protested querulously.

Miss Acaster ignored this. Hearing a lot of noise coming from higher up, she made her way up the escalator by the tumbled piles of books. Mortimer followed her hopefully, for he connected her in his mind with Arabel; they were always handing books to each other.

Sure enough, coming out on the roof, they found Arabel, Naughty Madge Owens, and the three boys.

"Kaaark!" said Mortimer joyfully on seeing Arabel, and he made his way to her as fast as he could without actually flying.

Then he noticed the hang-gliders, and was struck dumb with amazement and admiration. They were like nothing he had ever encountered.

"Dear me! Hang gliders – how very convenient," said Miss Acaster. "Could one of you boys take me as a passenger, do you think?"

"Blimey," muttered Bill, "how many *more* passengers are going to come up out of there?" He looked doubtfully at Miss Acaster, so tall and bony, and even more doubtfully at Rollo, who was big and heavy, even for a bloodhound.

Arabel leaned as far as she dared over the parapet, for she thought she could see her father and Chris, down below, coasting over the floods in Dave's dinghy.

"Pa! Chris! I'm up here, with Mortimer!" she called.

Arabel's voice was not very loud, but when Naughty Madge Owens yelled: "Hey, Mr Jones! Your daughter's up here!" both Chris and Mr Jones heard her, and waved, beaming.

A great roar of cheering went up also from all the boats, and from the people along Rumbury Wasteside. Papers were waved and ribbons were fluttered. Naughty Madge's fans had arrived.

"Now: who's going first?" asked Dave.

"I'll take Arabel and Mortimer," said Sandy.

He harnessed himself to his hang-glider. Then he buckled his belt round Arabel, passing one end of the belt through the hang-glider harness. He would have buckled Mortimer also, but Mortimer refused to be buckled.

"I'll just hold him," Arabel said.

"Mind you hold tight then," said Sandy.

He climbed on the parapet, jumped off, and floated gently down, gliding right across the floods to land on the dry ground in front of the public library.

Everybody cheered like mad.

Then Dave followed with Miss Acaster. He flatly refused to take Rollo, who remained on the roof howling heartbreakingly.

"I'll send somebody back for you right away, Rollo," called Miss Acaster.

Rollo looked and sounded as if he did not believe her.

Dave and Miss Acaster managed to glide even farther than Sandy had with Arabel,

perhaps because they were both heavier.
They landed by the gasworks. A crowd
rushed to welcome them, including some
police.

"I shall have to take you into custody,
Miss Acaster," said the Chief Constable of
Rumbury Town, as he had already to Sandy
and Arabel. "The charge is illegal entry
of private premises, and operating a
hang-glider in a built-up area."

Miss Acaster drew herself up to her full
height. Her eyes flashed.

She said: "I have been retrieving stolen
Council property! You will find a thousand

stolen library books inside that building. And I have personally apprehended the thieves; you will find them stapled to the floor. And these young people have been assisting me."

"Stapled to the floor, eh?" said the Chief Constable, scratching his head. He let the prisoners go again.

"Please send somebody over to rescue that bloodhound immediately," ordered Miss Acaster.

Now Bill Mulvey and Naughty Madge Owens came floating to the edge of the flood. This time the cheers were so deafening that the whole of Rumbury Town rang and shook and rocked. All her fans rushed to be first to greet Naughty Madge, who would certainly have been trampled to death if the Chief Constable hadn't thrust her into his enormous car.

"Hey! You police weren't a lot of help!"

Naughty Madge said tartly to the Chief Constable. "Kidnapped by a gang of mobsters and I didn't see *you* rushing to rescue me!"

"Who did rescue you, then, miss?"

"*She* did," said Naughty Madge, pointing to Arabel, who was being hugged by her father and Chris.

"And where are the miscreants who kidnapped you, then, miss?" said the Chief Constable, who didn't believe a word. He thought it was all a publicity stunt.

"I daresay they are still in that building," said Naughty Madge, adjusting her wig, for a lot of newspaper photographers were taking pictures.

"That building must be packed with criminals like a sardine tin," grumbled the Chief Constable. However he sent a boatful of armed police to investigate.

Arabel, Mortimer, Chris, and Mr Jones went home to breakfast, returning Sandy's boat on the way. Mrs Jones had just woken up. She was so pleased to see Arabel and Mortimer that she didn't make as much fuss as they expected; instead she scrambled a whole lot of eggs and made twelve pieces of toast.

The Hatmen were sent to prison.

Mr Beeline did not go to prison, but was given such a warning that he completely stopped stealing library books, and instead took to pinching police bollards and orange lights from pedestrian crossings.

Rumbury Tower Heights still stands empty and the bats are still in residence. Dave, Bill, and Sandy plan to have another go at hang-gliding from the top some time when the Chief Constable is engaged elsewhere.

Mortimer is very happy. He has ridden on the fountain *and* on a hang-glider; even more than he expected.

Naughty Madge Owens sent Arabel a brooch, and a T-shirt with her picture on it, autographed.

And, thank goodness, the trench along Rainwater Crescent has been filled in at last, so that Mr Jones can park his taxi in front of the house again.